Flip Your Coin

TO
ANNE
KEEP STAYING STRON
KEEP POSITIVE FOR DAVID
& POSITIVE FOR
God LOVES You

John P. Ogwu

To order additional copies of this book, contact:
Xlibris Corporation
0-800-644-6988
www.xlibrispublishing.co.uk
Orders@xlibrispublishing.co.uk
302806

Contents

DEDICATION

Flip Your Coin

This book is dedicated to my beautiful and wonderful mother who has always been my source of courage, persistence, and determination. She has shown great strength of character having been widowed twenty-two years ago, when I was just five years old. I love you Mother, always and forever.

*   *   *

Introduction

_____

We must use time wisely and forever realize that the time is always ripe to do right.—*Nelson Mandela*

* * *

Preface

There are many self-help books written by Authors that cut across the globe. But what you have here is more than a self-help guide. The author shows himself an original and creative thinker with a rare literary propensity. He succeeded in creating an active and effectual synergy between reality as it is and his life experiences. This is a book that is set to challenge, correct, advise, assist, counsel, prod, rejuvenate and consolidate you in your ardent search for relevance, success, progress and peace in a world that does not seem to give them. It is a plunge into the deepest recess of life to derive as it were those potent elements that define human life. It is an optimistic reading of the divine script pasted on the walls of existence. This book will long outlive the author !

Rev. Fr. Boniface Nkem Anusiem PhD.

*   *   *

Nigeria, one of the largest countries in Africa.

Chapter 1

Blame Game

All blame is a waste of time. No Matter how much fault you find with another, and regardless of how much you blame him, it will not change you. The only thing blame does is to keep the focus off you when you are looking for external reasons to explain your unhappiness or frustration. You may succeed in making another feel guilty about something by blaming him, but you wouldn't succeed in changing whatever it is about you that is making you unhappy....

—Wayne Dyer

Stop being a victim and start living like a winner and feel victorious. When things do not go as planned, instead of blaming ourselves, we tend to blame someone else for our own mishaps. True, the other person may have been involved in the whole incident; is it fair to always blame someone else when we are to blame as well?

Take, for example, from the Bible, the story of the fall of man in the Garden of Eden. Eve was deceived by the snake; she took the apple from the tree of knowledge, ate it, and gave it to her husband, Adam, to eat. When God asked Adam what had happened, he blamed Eve, for she gave him the apple to eat. Eve blamed the serpent for deceiving her. Why did I bring this story up? Because I want you to remember where the blame game had begun. Since the beginning of time, whether you believe it or not, we tend to blame other people when we are in the wrong ourselves. Wake up! It is time for us to quench the thirst of blaming other people and start taking the responsibility for the things that are going on in our lives and facing whatever challenges that come our way. Telling you to wake up means that a part of you is sleeping and needs to be awakened. That part of you is the part that you have successfully locked away knowingly or unknowingly because you lack self-confidence. Listen carefully to whatever ideas you wished to explore, however, have abandoned due to someone telling you it was not good enough—perhaps, the goal which you wanted to accomplish—you were discouraged from taking action. It's time you polish those ideas and begin putting them into action and believing in yourself. It could be the deciding factor in life whether you will be happy or regretful and resentful in life. We are all spiritual beings going through a human experience; having been created into the human beings that we are, we also have the ability to create. We have been given that power on our journey to this planet. It is within us, and it enables us to become whomever we choose to become on this good earth, only if we are ready to make great use of it.

Have you decided what role you are playing in this grand scheme of life? Are you a generalist or a specialist? Where do you belong? The answer lies within you and not outside of you. Go right inside you, and find out.

This blame game that you have been playing, consciously or unconsciously, has to stop with you today. What does not and should not concern you is what other people do because they are not living in you. They do not want to move on with their life as you do. Who is reading this book now? You. Let us focus on you.

Do you want to change for the better? Do you want to succeed and live the life you deserve? Then you need to stop blaming people when things do not go as you would have hoped. Invest that energy on making things happen with persistence and perseverance. I promise you, by the time you have finished reading and applying the guidelines as stated in this book, your thinking will have changed from blaming to being in total control. What you will focus on will be different, and your mind-set will be renewed each day when you read these pages.

There is only one rule to the blame game; blame someone or something else. It is a rule we have adopted since childhood and has accompanied us throughout adulthood. I am quite certain and confident in saying that when we were little children and broken something, we did not think to blame ourselves for it falling over; we threw the blame on the inanimate object that fell over "on its own," even though we were the ones who ran through the house and into the table. Well, although we may have not blamed someone, we did blame the table. Similar stories are out there; they keep coming in our teens, twenties, thirties, forties, fifties, and so on—when will it stop? For some of us, it never stops. The game gets more classified. The blame game is an attitude that stops us from taking control of our life because we are always having the second or third party at fault for the mistakes we have made.

Some of the people who tend to get the most blame are our family members. If anything they have said has stopped us from doing something, we blame them.

"Mother said this. So it is her fault. That is why I did not pursue that."

"Dad was not in my life, so it is his fault why I am not doing well."

In some people's lives, the examples are true statements. However, for a lot of us, these examples become excuses not to move forward in life, become stagnant, and to keep making accusations.

This theory can also happen the other way around. Your mother or father may have discouraged you from visiting family members. The easy way out is not taking responsibility for the results in your life. I am sure you have stories to tell as to why things are not complete in your life, or why you are not living your dreams. Let me give you a hand:

"He did it!"

"It's because my mother I didn't attend to a university."

"It's because my father doesn't know how to read and write."

"It's because my credit card got lost."

"There was no money!"

"There was no role model in my life." "How can I go out when it's raining?"

Yes, you might even blame the weather for not taking action. Yet if you were just called on the phone and informed that you had just won $2 million, would you for a second let the weather stop you? Think about it. We can be like that at times, but why let simple things stop us from moving forward? It does not impress anyone, knowing that you did not finish something of importance because of the weather. If your parents do not have the qualifications, be it Dad or Mom or even both, why should that stop you from achieving? Make the move and wake up!

You must move forward with a better frame of mind and quit pointing fingers. If you are late for work or an event, there is always a potential second party that can get the blame card, even though you may have left the house late that day.

You have to understand that it is not what happens to you that determines your future, but it is what you do with what happens that determines the major part of your future. The result is how you are able to deal with every incident that occurs in your life.

Let us take, for example, tardiness. If you find yourself using the same excuses and blaming certain situations for arriving late, then you need to make a change now. If it means getting up earlier, then you have to do that. Basically, you have to do something different in order for you to achieve a new result. You cannot keep leaving the house late and expect to drive straight through until your destination.

Just ponder these type of events over the last three months. Get a piece of paper and write down a list of all the people, things and events you have blamed. Do these things seem insignificant? Try not to convince yourself that they lack importance; everything is important. The point is to make a change so that you no longer have to blame events, people, things etc for your shortcomings. My mentor, the late Jim Rohn, said, "what you have in your life and where you are at today is because you have attracted these things to yourself." It is time for personal development. Wake up from your slumber.

"Blame this or blame that" is a program in your subconscious mind, and it manifests itself every time you think of excuses. This self-destructive game can be uprooted from your life in a very constructive way when you begin to be consciously aware of its damage to your life. Your mind-set has to believe that to every problem, there is a solution waiting, and the solution starts with you and the way you process your thoughts.

You must change the way you think and the way you take information in. The information you take in must only be positive because like attracts like, and everything is energy. John F. Kennedy said, "One person can make a difference and every person should try."

Now is the time to make hay while the sun shines, take back the power of your mind, and control your life the way you want it. Now is the time that you must abandon the blame game that you have embraced for such a long while. I am calling to your attention the freedom to live your life just as you want it. Free yourself from all sorts of blame, only if you are ready to let them go forever.

Now is the time to liberate yourself from mental slavery. Do you think because there are no more visible shackles on your hands, that it means all of the shackles have been removed? What about the shackles of your mind? Well, think about it, because it is within your capability to remove and bury the shackles of your mind.

I used to blame events, situations, and even God for the backlashes that used to occur in my life until I found out that the answer lay within me. For majority of people, a significant portion of their lives has been involved in judging, criticizing, and blaming the government policies, parents, friends, and religious leaders for why they have not achieved their dreams in life. The willpower to take action shatters the prevailing power of the blame game and brings you success. When you know what you want to achieve, then you can unlock your potentials from within. Your attitude will begin to develop new traits, which will render the game powerless.

As you read this, your subconscious mind is kicking in slowly, telling you this is not worth your time. I urge you to allow the thoughts to keep flowing. No more blaming! Wake up and understand that you have to make a daily assessment of yourself through your personal life philosophy to begin making changes that will help you to evolve into the self that you wish. Recognize the thoughts, that have been running your entire being and life. Will you keep transferring this self-defeating program from your generation to generation, or are you putting an end to it now? If you want to put this program to rest, then the only way forward, is to cease repeating the same mistakes over and over again. Learn from your mistakes today.

As you read through these pages, your mind might be open (bravo). In contrast, you might be having doubts, regarding the benefits you might derive by the time you get to the last page. Are you not already placing negative thoughts on yourself, causing you to not move forward? I urge you to sprint into the new mind-set that awaits you. I want you to know that when you begin working on your attitude, you will be amazed at the immediate effect it has on your life.

There is a special doctor that heals this self-deficiency. The specialist is you! You are your own doctor. Why? Because you are the only one that has the password to your mind's activation. You are the only one accepting and rejecting thoughts that empower your empire (body). You are the only one who can create vision, dream dreams, and make them materialize. People may say things to you, but it is your choice whether to hold on to them or not. Don't wish things were easier, but wish you were better. Don't wish for less problems, but wish for more skills. Don't wish for less challenge, but wish for more wisdom. It is time you start working on habits, and everything else will change for you.

*   *   *

Chapter 2

Wake Up Now

Life is one big road with lots of signs. So when you riding through the ruts, don't complicate your mind. Flee from hate, mischief and jealousy. Don't bury your thoughts, put your vision to reality. Wake Up and Live!

—Bob Marley

It is time to rise and shine! Here is the time to think deeply about all the things you have heard, judged, and acted upon—whether they are fact or fiction and whether they have been a positive influence in your life. Let nothing stop you from taking immediate action now, especially even self-denial. It is time for you to discard the thoughts that have no use anymore in your life and replace them with ideas and thoughts that will awaken your mind and make you realize that you have been the one holding yourself back all this precious while. Do you remember the old clothes you wore when you were five years old? You may no longer wear them anymore, but some of you might see them from time to time in your parent's attic. At the moment you do see them, these old clothes tend to bring up nostalgic thoughts of times when you were content and without worry and always ready to find out what was around the corner. At that moment in your life, you never let anything stop you. That attitude can still operate in your life today. Today is a new dawn. Today is a morning of change. The younger *you*, who, enjoyed the constant new ventures while growing up has fallen asleep. The *you* that lives today can still find those ventures, but instead of those ventures being in the form of playing all day, you need to find them in different ways that are consistent with what your life is about today. You need to pull exhilaration from what your purpose in life is, your goals, vision map and dreams. Although gaining fulfillment as an adult may not be as appealing as playing all day long, in the end, it is much more self-fulfilling and longer lasting. You need to start living in the joys and accomplishments of today. If there is a dream that you have been nurturing but not living out, now is the time to step out with courage, and explore it to the fullest!

Start thinking over what you have created in the form of excuses for yourself and how they have stopped you from moving forward in particular aspects of your life. This exercise must be done in a solitary place. Even Jesus Christ had to go off to pray alone on the mountains when things got too hectic in town. Why? Because he needed time to gather his thoughts and recharge for the journey that was ahead of him. Do you ever take the time to reflect and review on the things that are happening in your life?

I urge you to go somewhere where you can be alone and think without interruption—a place where you can find solace with and within yourself. Make notes of some important thoughts that will be vital to you when you get back home.

Nelson Mandela said, "we must use time wisely and forever realize that the time is always ripe to do right."

Your time to arise and shine.

Our body is a powerful force of its own that receives information with our five sensory organs and stores them for later use. Have you ever heard someone say, "my life flashed before my eyes?" That is the body recalling a situation to pull getting them out of a life-threatening problem. In the same way, we tend to hang on to things that do not help us out of problems and only create more difficulty for us. While you are in your quiet time, decode the thoughts, sounds, and emotions which are no longer relevant to what you want to achieve today, with patience and perseverance.

Nelson Mandela said, "for to be free is not merely to cast off one's chain, but to live in a way that respects and enhances the freedom of others."

Before we enhance the freedom of others, let us free ourselves first.

I no longer want you to wake up to thoughts of the past that drag you down to a pit of despair. I want you to wake up to a brand-new way of thinking. Think about this: if you had only three more months on this beautiful planet to live, what is that burning desire within you that you want to achieve? What would make you drop everything and go after it and achieve it? Now write it down because you have just found your passion and purpose in life. Now you can remove the three months and see the beautiful years ahead of you, which should give you a new zest for life. You will find inner peace when you achieve this burning desire because more doors will open once you have accomplished this task. It does not matter what it is; what does matter is that it must come from within you. It is the sleeping part of you waiting to wake up.

Let us think about our parents and guardians for a minute. Some of you lucky few had the following question posed to you: What do you want to be when you grow up? On the other side, there are those of us who were told what we were going to be. You know the cliché jobs: accountant, doctor, lawyer, nurse, Rev. Father, sailor, dentist, Engineer and so on.

Let me offer you this short story about myself. When I was seven years old, my beloved mother began grooming me for the profession, which my late father did not accomplish. She said that since my father could not achieve this goal, I was in the best position as the first son to achieve this dream. The profession my father could not complete and the one my mother suggested for me was to become a Roman Catholic priest.

I can say with strict confidence that this was not my dream, goal, purpose, or desire,. My mother played the role of both parents in my family. With that said, and being only a young boy of seven, I obeyed her with sincerity and received this dream with an open heart. I believed it was the best and only thing on this planet, and I believed my mother wanted the best for me. She suggested I become a Roman Catholic Father and that became my focus. Hindsight 20-20 it was a spiritual journey. While I was in the seminary I was choosen as a pueri cantores in representing Africa together with my colleagues I met the late Pope John Paul II at the Vatican City, Rome, Italy, during the Jubilee year 2000. Shortly after this, I determined that this was not what I wanted to be in life. I was nurturing her dream. Had my mother asked me what I wanted to be, I would have told her that my burning desire and dream was to become a pilot. This dream stemmed from the moment I can first recall playing with a huge toy airplane in our backyard. I kept visualizing myself flying this airplane. I imagined I would one day be the one piloting it in the sky. I was never asked what my own thoughts were about my future.

Forging on with my mother's desire for me to become a Roman Catholic Reverend Father. At the age of ten, I took my first entrance examination and was on my way to seminary school. After spending a good number of my teen years in the seminary, I came to understand that Catholic priests do not get married. The lid of this dream finally blew open.

I remember discussing with a friend at the seminary that I wanted to have children of my own and a beautiful family just like my father had. I also knew that I would, out of human nature, want to make love with my other significant other. However, that was against the laws of the Roman Catholic church. That was when I began to take total control of my life. I came to the conclusion and made the firm decision that although the seminary had been the spiritual foundation in my life, it was not where I was meant to be.

I loved my mother dearly. I always would, but deep in my heart, I found myself asking if I was here to make her happy over my own happiness. Have you ever felt that you are merely pleasing others? Have you ever found yourself asking this same or a similar question?

It takes courage and self-confidence to make your own decisions in life. When I finally decided to reveal this to my mother, I automatically thought she would disagree with my chosen path. I was surprised to find that she was of the same opinion. She honored my choice to leave the priesthood and was happy and very supportive of me to continue my life's journey as I saw fit.

Yes, I am well aware that you may have not expected that ending. I, as well, was entirely gobsmacked! I am also aware that the ride and changes may not be as smooth for you as they were for me, but with perseverance, the breakthrough is yours.

I am on a journey to my own childhood dreams. I am completing flying lessons and becoming a professional pilot. My heart's desires are materializing into my desired lifestyle. I am taking charge of my destiny and creating the life I have always dreamt of living. It feels great becoming what your heart and soul want you to become and going after what you want instead of what you feel is best in order to please others

Ask yourself these questions: whose dream are you living? what are you doing with your life now? whose desires are you fulfilling? Here is the moment and time when you determine the things that you want to achieve in life. Back in chapter one, we discussed the blame game. It's time to evolve into the full potential of your being. We are spiritual beings going through a human experience.

I believe now you are half-awake, but guess what, by the time you reach the last page of this book, you would be fully awake and ready for the new beginnings for the next phase of your life. This is the moment of rebirth; planet earth is our playground.

Think about this; you are the producer, boss, publisher, storyteller of your life. Therefore, it's a win-win situation.

Here is the place and time where you are in tune with your higher self, God, the creator, committing to doing what you love doing and becoming the best at it. I believe you want to be a specialist instead of a generalist. In brief, you are familiar with general practitioner (GP), and you trust his decisions and are prepared to put your precious life in his hands when you are ill. What if you found out that your GP is also a chef at your favorite restaurant. Would you become skeptical about his ability as a doctor? Yes, you would because you believed that his focus was on his medical profession. Does that say anything about you?

Wake up to your dreams; they are achievable.

Wake up to your passion; they are achievable.

Wake up to your own reality; everything is possible.

Wake up to your inner strength and potentials.

Do not make your life decisions based on what others think is right for you or what your parents dream as yours. Do not make decisions based on your present bank balance but rather make decisions based on that which you know would make you a happy individual. Always remember your parents' dreams are totally different from yours. In a quiet place, think about that which would bring you closer to your dreams and plan your goals step by step, and you would find yourself achieving your dreams in an accurate and timely manner.

*   *   *

Chapter 3

No Excuses

Ninety-nine percent of the failures come from people who have the habit of making excuses.

—George Washington Carver

Having now read both previous chapters carefully and now that your conscious mind and subconscious mind have agreed to stop the blame game, you are beginning to awake even further now. Right now, I will help you to see who you truly are and not who you think you are or who your subconscious mind tells you you are. Why have you remained in the same position, same hustle, and same struggle day in and day out? Have you done this to make ends meet or perhaps to be comfortable? Guess what, comfortability sucks. Making ends meet . . . well, they will never meet. You are not living within your means but are trying to delude yourself into mediocrity.

I know sometimes in your private moments you sit down and blame God—LOL! I was in the habit of blaming God. This has got nothing to do with, God, Allah, or the universe. It has got a lot to do with you and you alone. Refer to Chapter 1 (Blame Game). Everything you need, in order to become who you want to, is already within you. What you see on the inside is what will manifest on the outside.

You are the one putting the handcuffs on yourself and stepping on the brakes in your life all the time. I know you are thinking, "How can that be?" Reflect on the past and realize that you are not where you *want* to be because you have not allowed yourself to do so.

You can deny this, yet, accept it and look forward to the solution as you read on. In the same way you get viruses on computers and mobile phones, you also get so-called "viruses" in your mind. I want you to know that the viruses that corrupt the mind are the excuses that we plant in there ourselves, which stem from our own limiting beliefs.

I also believe, however, that you now know how to burn or delete those excuses. It is now time to get another clean sheet of paper and write down the list of things that would propel you toward those goals and dreams of yours.

Notes

<u>Notes</u>

<u>Notes</u>

<u>Notes</u>

Make sure that you have that paper in your wallet or purse because that is your winning lottery ticket, for you and you alone. Think of it as the navigational system in your car. Without it, you are lost and stuck in confusion and frustration, and that is how you will continue to feel if you do not have goals set in place and a vision map driving you to your dreams.

I know you want to be successful. Yes! You want to be a winner. Yes!

You want to take total control of your life now. Yes!

You want to be in the driving seat of your life. Yes!

But guess what? It is all but mere wishes without action. Wishing we can change is the beginning, but now wish must be translated into activity and inspiration and affirmation must lead to discipline. We can affirm that we need to change but we must now form new habits. You will forever remain stuck with your wishes, and wishes alone unless you take instant action to transform your dream into reality as stated above.

Your life can only be enhanced if you follow these simple steps. Once completed, your life will become more effective, prosperous, and joyous, and happiness would be yours forever.

Those of you who have driven any automobile may have an idea of what moves it and what slows it down. I want to ask you about the brake that slows the car down: is it an external force or an internal force?

I think it is an internal force, as well as the accelerator is also an internal force. However, which of them are you applying in your life right now? Answer that for yourself because whichever you are applying is the catalyst (cause) of where you are today in life.

Finally, you have decided to hold on to the brakes (fear and excuses), which have been your own personal source of motivation, and you keep looking for outside forces to help you take your foot off the brakes. The brakes are the excuses or viruses that your conditioned mind keeps producing for you out of fear. At some point, you must realize, that the quiet voice awaiting us from within, is all we need.

Exercise: Drop this book now and get a clean sheet of paper and write down the goal or dream that has always been on your mind to achieve.

Notes

<u>Notes</u>

<u>Notes</u>

<u>Notes</u>

<u>Notes</u>

Now write down on another sheet of clean white paper all the junk excuses that have been stopping you from taking action.

What I want you to do now is to burn those excuses that have kept you captive for however many number of years and robbed you of living your dream life. These excuses have produced the tape recorder in your head, mentally giving you a million excuses why you cannot make it in life, blah, blah, blah! This behavior pattern has caused you to be handicapped (mentally).

Take hold of your dreams, goals, and aspirations. Write down all the positive actions that you need to get your mind, body, soul, and spirit in motion right now.

<u>Notes</u>

<u>Notes</u>

<u>Notes</u>

You can lead a horse to water, but you cannot make it drink. Now you can lead a horse to water and be sure it will drink with the following technique! Give the horse some salty food, and when it gets to the water, it will automatically drink, drink, and drink. Does this ring a bell in your own ears? If it does, then I believe you are ready to release the brakes completely.

Susan Jeffers said, "Feel the fear and do it anyway." That is the same principle that guides rich and wealthy individuals. You must be willing to feel fear and do it anyways, because the more uncomfortable you are, the better and the higher you will be able to climb and become that person you wish to be.

One of the great weaknesses of our society today is the growing attitude of victimization. Many people claim themselves to be victims of some outside force. James Allen says a "creature of outside conditions" we have no power. We have given over the power in our life to the circumstances. The longer we give power to our circumstances the worse our circumstances become.

Albert Einstein said, "The same mind that created the problem cannot solve the same problem."

Now it is time for you to take action with the law of concentration! Now you will begin creating the things that will enhance your life and bring you towards your destined goals and dreams.

You are the only one controlling your life. By failing to plan, you are planning to fail. Thus, you are setting yourself up for automatic failure. I believe I am speaking the truth here and now. You can begin dwelling on the positives in your life, keeping your conscious mind focused, and what you want to begin in your life will start to move toward you. (Henry David Thoreau said, "When one advances in the directions of his dreams and endeavors to live the life which he has imagined, he will meet with a success unexpected in common hours.") You are on your way to more success and prosperity in every facets of your life now.

Excuses are the virus that corrupts your mind from achieving your own goals.

> "An excuse is worse and more terrible than a lie, for an excuse is a lie guarded."
> —**Pope John Paul II**

*   *   *

Chapter 4

Recreate Your Life

"Remind yourself. Nobody built like you, you design yourself." You are an original. Nobody can offer what you can offer. You are also the one that defines who you are, not everybody else's opinion of you."

—Jay Z (Shawn Carter)

The power to create your life lies in your hands. There are two different kinds of people: those who wait for life to happen to them and those who create their own lives.

Whomever you create in your mind is who you become in reality; you are the architect of your own life.

Some Lyrics from the song called the Power of the dream by Celine Dion,

"Deep within each heart,
There lies a magic spark,
That lights the fire of our imagination . . .

Your mind will take you far,
The rest is just pure heart,
You'll find your fate is all your own creation."

Once you create firm foundations in your mental world, that is what you will eventually give birth to in your real world. When you create the opposite, it will result in a world of poverty from within. Why beat yourself up when you can go back inside and create something a lot better? Well, ninety-nine percent of this comes from the accumulation of fear that has been in you since your childhood.

Your mental world is part of the workshop of your dreams and goals in life. Have you asked yourself what is it you would love to create in life? What is the beautiful music that stirs deep within your soul ?Who do you want to become in future? Whichever seed you sow today is what grows to be the "bigger you" tomorrow; there is no magic to this. You cannot sow corn and expect onions. Well, that is what you have been doing.

The majority of people want to remain the same person that they are now. They are scared of change on every level. Besides that, when they were growing up, they never knew about fear, but now they are cooperating with the dragon (fear) that controls their entire being.

Are you living your dreams or are you dreaming your dreams? Take a good look at everything that is around you presently . . . . guess what it was someday someones dream. Dreams are the seedlings of realities. You can do either—live your dreams or wish your dreams.

Where do you belong? The good news is, wherever you belong, you can identify this to yourself and you alone.

Taking total control of your life from this very moment places you in a very good position to experience a greater freedom, and express who you choose to become! If I ask you what kind of lifestyle you want to live, only you would know! Besides that, it is good to visualize your vision. Perhaps, taking action and writing your vision, which is a clearly defined goal, task, and step toward the realization of your dreams, is a major process. Getting to work on every precise aspect of your goal, step-by-step, leads you to your paradise land.

Remember, the majority of people just choose to live in mediocrity at the bottom level of the triangle (which is the most populated). The vision now is for you to identify where you want to be, and how you get there is another aspect of the journey.

You have to set yourself on the path of success. Besides that, you must acknowledge the paths of failure. You have taken in the past. There will be failures along the way, and it takes brave, courageous, and resilient souls to pick themselves up and continue to soar until they get to the dream that they have set for themselves. At the end of your life, what would you like to say on your deathbed? The answer is yours. Take charge now so you can have the most beautiful smile on your face, knowing fully well that you achieved all that you have set out for yourself.

Do you have a huge dream for your life, and you find that your friends are trying to sabotage you. Do you find them laughing at you? Let me tell you for free, that you are 50 percent along your journey to achieving your success! Those mockers that do not have a dream are laughing their way to permanent failure in every aspect of their lives! They have automatically given up on life, and also, they are the types of people we spoke about in the beginning of the book: those who wait for life to happen to them. Abraham Lincoln said, "If you keep waiting in life, those who hustle would have gotten everything. What you get are the crumbs of what they have left behind.?" This is the point at which you should understand that you are on a different vibrational level.

Our determination and zeal creates the kind of life that we live. Whatever you are able to do, do it now!

Johann Wolfgang von Goethe said, "Boldness has genius, power and magic in it. Begin it now."

The secret of happiness is freedom. The secret of freedom is courage.

You can be mentally free, which in turn creates financial freedom! We are all responsible for creating the kind of life that we have chosen to live. How do you choose the kind of life that you desire?

Well, I know you are ready to learn this. Check it out; the answer is within you—by listening to that quiet voice that never has enough time to express itself before the conditioned mind takes over.

You carry the answer within you everywhere you go. A saying from Buddha is "When the student is ready to learn, then the teacher will appear." The antidote is that you do not need to wait until you are financially free and begin practicing mental freedom, which automatically changes your pattern of thought and begins to direct your life toward your destined goal and passion in life. Blaise Pascal said, "all of man's troubles come from not knowing how to sit still, alone in a room." The higher your self-belief, the greater the power to transform your vision into reality is.

Thousands of candles can be lit from a single candle, but the life of the candle will not be shortened. Happiness never decreases by being shared. For every minute you are angry, you lose sixty seconds of happiness.

> "Don't let the opinions of the average man sway you. Dream, and he thinks you're crazy. Succeed, and he thinks you're lucky. Acquire wealth, and he thinks you're greedy. Pay no attention. He simply doesn't understand."
>
> —Robert G. Allen

$$*\quad*\quad*$$

Chapter 5

Think Bigger

"Think BIG goals and win BIG success, Big ideas and big plans are often easier-certainly no more difficult-than small ideas and small plans"

David Joseph Swartz

Now in this chapter, I want you to make some notes, and draw what you envision to be your dream life. When you are done, I want you to increase the drawing sevenfold and ride on that wave. "Feel the fear and do it anyways."

<u>Notes</u>

<u>Notes</u>

<u>Notes</u>

You may have heard of the saying that goes like this: "If you aim for the moon, at least if you miss you will land amongst the stars." Now, you must ask yourself one question: What have you been thinking about, and where are you now in your life? Just remember, if you think small, you will become small.

Perhaps, you do not participate in increasing or expanding your thought patterns like those who think as huge as the elephant and end up becoming a lion. So, now I am challenging your thought pattern to think bigger than you have ever thought of before, because someone on this planet has accomplished whatever you are thinking or dreaming about already. Is it that the thought of thinking bigger than yourself scares you? I guess that is what has kept you in your comfort zone, and you keep finding yourself doing the same thing over and over again.

Here is a method for enhancing your life in every aspect of your being, which includes your net worth.

"All the resources we need are in our mind."—Theodore Roosevelt.

The Magic is in you. "When he realizes that he is a creative power, and that he may command the hidden soil and seeds of his being out of which circumstances grow; he then becomes the rightful master of himself" James Allen.

Soon you will begin to see how things turn up in your life. Remember, whatever you reap is a result of what you have sown in the past; what you reap in the future is what you sow now.

Once you are able to think bigger, you will begin to act bigger and create big things in every aspect of your life. It takes self-determination and courage to deliver your thought into reality.

The ability to think bigger than your life is the realization of a desired goal. We lose definite purpose because we don't even think at all. You are who you become with the outcome of your mind.

The most dynamic function of every living being is the utilization of the mind in its complete objectives. From this very moment, you can actually understand that the key to unlock your mind lies in the power of thinking bigger than your being, which helps you to achieve more in life. It is very essential that you open yourself up to more opportunities for accomplishment.

IF YOU ARE GOING TO THINK AT ALL THINK BIG.
—DONALD J. TRUMP

*   *   *

Chapter 6

Be Courageous

"The most courageous act is still to think for yourself. Aloud."

—**Coco Chanel**, fashion design icon.

Here is a typical example of a courageous act: Mohamed Bouazizi, a Tunisian street vendor, sacrificed himself for freedom and dignity, which is a symbol of eternity. Before late Pope John Paul II passed away, he kept emphasizing on the urgency for Africa to have courage and rise up.

"Courage is the resistance to fear, mastery of fear, not absence of fear."—Mark Twain

This creates the ability and the potential that lies within us all. Look deep within yourself; there is a huge potential and talent that resides within you, and whether you believe it or not, it is there. It takes courage to develop this talent, and guess what? Every dream and wish you have ever had for yourself will come to pass. This energy lies in each and every one of us. Why have you decided to save it and not use it? When will you bring it to work? You keep saying tomorrow. Look—does your tomorrow ever come? Procastination is life treathning according to my mentor Jim Rohn. It is time to forget about what you say, and watch the things you are doing. Our mouths are always very quick to speak, but our actions are saying things differently.

Do you trust yourself? Do you believe in yourself? Well, if you did, you would be moving toward your dream. Who says you cannot achieve and become whatever you want to become in life? You! Just you!

You have the ability, but you allow fear to take control and keep judging your life. If you do not even believe in yourself; how much more would you expect from the government?

I want you to know that each and every one of you has got the ferociousness of a lion, which is why I want you to take this exercise very seriously.

I want you to take a day off for yourself and go to any zoo that has got a lion and a tiger. Take your time to study these beautiful big cats. When you get home, write down the qualities of these cats, and implement them in your life. The result is amazing. Moreover, when you take children there, who are innocent and happy, they even want to go close to these cats. However, due to all the programming that you have had throughout your life, it stops you from taking a step further. Look, you do not trust yourself Irrespective of how many more people you meet, how many more relationships you have, and so on, when you lack courage in your life, you are automatically locked into the prison of fear, which is within you. It is time for you to stop wishing and start making these wishes reality.

Take another example. Once little children decide to begin walking, understand the fact that they have already watched you, the adult, walking around them. They have automatically programmed themselves to do exactly what you are doing, believing they must achieve the same. They are copying from you. No matter how many times they fall, that never is their concern; their minds are on the end result, which is getting up and walking. That is how you ended up walking just before you began to program fear into yourself about every little thing. Children are resilient souls.

If you are downloading a program on your computer and it is not compatible, what do you do? Automatically, you have it deleted! Now why do you hold on to dear life, those programs your parents have implemented in your life? Because those programs have been passed down for generations, and they are not compatible with your life. Stand, take a hold of courage, and begin to shape your life.

*   *   *

Chapter 7

Faith

Take the first step in faith. You don't have to see the whole staircase, just take the first step.

—Martin Luther King, Jr.

From my own experience, faith is mostly applied and potent when that surge of desperate actions just happens. These are vulnerable moments when we want immediate answers to challenges that we are facing in a particular moment or at any given occasion. These are the attributes whereby you are totally confident of the assistance and help that is being rendered to you in any form.

Here is the time, whereby, you are no longer relying on what you know but on God, the invisible force, superpower, divine master, the higher self, high intelligence, and so on. It all depends on whichever one you have been programed with since birth. The choice is yours.

In situations like this, you have two options and one decision to make.

The first choice that comes to 99.9 percent of human beings are thoughts based on fears of the worst possible things that could happen to them. But let me tell you something that will be very vital to you for the rest of your life. If at this point of vulnerability, you think optimistic and positive thoughts about the situation, you will 101 percent of the time, get a positive outcome.

In my own experience, it took me a while to master myself, my emotions and the situations that arose in my life, however I am still a life long learner Amazing miracles occur when one is able to recognize that we are part of this wonderful universe with plenty of opportunities. Is is so, because it is at this point that we are open to see these miracles. Believe me, every solution to a masterminded challenge lies in the single power of your thought.

Henceforth, at this point, I would urge you to focus on your highest goal, dream, or wish, and see how that feeling transforms your life immediately. The universe will present you with multiple opportunities that guide you toward that desired destination, which will manifest fruitfully in your life.

The reason why the opposite happens to 99.9 per cent of people is because they are too busy focusing on the worst thing that would happen to them. They eventually attract worst, and it materializes in their lives. Remember like attracts like.

This is not one's fault, I must say. Many of us have been programmed or conditioned from the time we were born to expect the worst in times of trials and tribulations. This course of action determines the make or break point of our lives. However, the good news is that we have the power of choice and can make a different decision.

Instead of allowing that monster called fear (false expectations appearing real) to take the driver's seat, it is time you allow courage to take control and drive you towards your desired outcome. Practice makes perfect.

When fear is substituted with faith and belief, optimal results are what you get out of these situations. Only one percent of every human being is programmed to think in this manner. These people arecalled the wealthy warriors." We are part of a divine source of unlimited power. Creators of our own experience" T Harv Eker.

This is the reason why I gave you the practice in Chapter 4 to visit the zoo, and specifically, visit the big cats (lions and tigers). Study them for an hour, write down your experiences, and go home and analyze what you have seen. Finally, incorporate those lessons into achieving your goals. The result will be magic.

*   *   *

Chapter 8

Love

I believe that every single event in life happens in an opportunity to choose love over fear.

—Oprah Winfrey

There is a book out there called "the law of divine compensation" by Marianne Williamson. The title pretty much say's it all, Yes! Here is a paragraph in the book as I quote !

"Love makes us wake up in the morning with a sense of purpose and a flow of creative ideas. Love floods our nervous system with positive energy, making us far more attractive to prospective employers, clients, and creative partners. Love fills us with a powerful charisma, enabling us to produce new ideas and new projects, even within circumstances that seem to be limited. Love leads us to atone for our errors and clean up the mess when we've made mistakes. Love leads us to act with impeccability, integrity, and excellence. Love leads us to serve, to forgive, and to hope. Those things are the opposite of a poverty consciousness; they're the stuff of spiritual wealth creation."

Love is spiritual, while sex is biological.

Love is my religion. Does your religion help you keep your own mind positive? All you need to become who you truly are is for you to love yourself, which has a tendency to come last on our to-do-list. Love is the act of showing affection to yourself before extending this act to someone else. If you cannot love yourself, there is no way you can love someone else. We should endeavor to apply this love on ourselves. If you do not love yourself, from where are you going to get confidence, hope, and faith? When we do not love ourselves, this beautiful and most powerful energy eludes us. It does see us breaking up from relationships with family, partners, friends, and colleagues. The act of sharing this beautiful energy stems from within us.

Love is patient, love is kind, love is faithful, love is compassionate, love is fearless, love is joyful, love is honest, love is forever, and love is yours and mine to share in blissful abundance.

Unconditionally and finally, love is you and me from the divine universe.

Love is the most powerful and potent energy on earth. This planet was created out of this blissful energy, love; while on it, we can only enjoy ourselves with the use of this energy. It begins when you start loving yourself.

As you continue to send out love, the energy returns to you in a regenerating spiral. As love accumulates, it keeps your system in balance and harmony. "Love is the tool, and more love is the end product" Sara Paddison.

Here is a short story : There is a great definition from the "*Psychology of Achievement Classic*" by Brian Tracy. The infant grief-death syndrome—they took children who were newborn and divided them into groups and brought to state hospitals. The first group of children was given continual holding, touching, and emotional support and talked to, sung to, and given warmth. The second group of children had their diapers (Pampers) changed and were never held, sung to, or received emotional support. The experiment had to be stopped due to grave ethical reason, but it was too late. Ninety per cent of the children in the second group died of grief in the first ninety days after birth. This has been called the infant grief-death syndrome.

If we could rise one generation with unconditional love, there would be abundant love. We need to teach this generation of children from day one that they are responsible for their lives. We all need love to grow our heart and soul just like we need water for our daily bath. If you do not think that love for oneself or others matters, please look around at the people who do not show affection or love to others. Do you enjoy being in the company of such a person who does not care about you? Equally, people who do not love themselves are hard to be around because they carry an aura of low energy vibration.

The word *tough* should never be associated with *love*. Tough love! It is a typical example of what happened to the second group of children during the infant grief-death syndrome. Please endeavor to keep the energy of unconditional love flowing regardless of any circumstance you find yourself. If you are not feeding your spouse and children with unconditional love, you are starving them from the fuel of life that would propel them in achieving their desired and destined goal in life. For you to achieve and reach your full potential in life, love is a prerequisite in every facets of your life. It will germinate and grow beautifully, and when the harvest is ready, who would reap the fruits? You will.

When we are capable enough of loving every fibre of our being without any remorse, only then can we love ourselves without any form of judgment and completely love them just the way we love ourselves. Those of you who are married and those who have been in a beautiful, loving relationship can testify to what I am saying. However for those of you who are yet to be in any sort of relationship, the magic is to begin loving oneself with a new mind-set, and you would be drawn to the love of your life only if you remain true to yourself. An anonymous philosopher quotes, "It was a great surprise to me when I discovered that most of the ugliness I saw in others was but a reflection of my own nature."

When you have one rotten apple in a basket of hundred apples and one goes rotten, what happens to the remaining apples automatically with time? It all goes rotten. When there is a part of your being that unconsciously you do not like, it does affect the remaining part of your body. For example, when you have toothache, do you hear the hand saying "I am not involved"? Sure, the entire body is involved. That's why you have to love every fiber of your being truly.

The more you value yourself, the more you will be able to value other people. Abundant love is available to you by putting these exercises to work today. If you are not loving, you are sleeping; if a plant is not growing, it is dying. This beautiful energy is always available to everyone at will.

Ask yourself this question: when you were born, was it out of love or hate? Were your parents hating each other or loving each other? By the laws of love, we are constantly creating. While by the opposite, we are destroying. Once again, where do you belong? Remember, there is no middle ground here, which is where we can try to hide at times. Do not be in a hurry to answer the question. We shall see where you belong as time ticks on smoothly.

"You will discover that unconditional love is millions of miles past falling in love with anyone or anything. When you make that one effort to feel compassion instead of blame or self-blame, the heart opens again and continues opening" Sara Paddison.

Love rules my world. What rules your world? The reason while individuals cheat on their partners is simply because they do not love themselves. If you completely love yourself and you know the odds are very slim for you to get infected with HIV AIDS, you would not take the risk of bringing that to your partner (Wife / Husband). Love is the bridge between where we are at now and our destination in life. The acts of self-love increases; self-confidence and self-worth automatically increase your net worth. For more inspiration and teachings on this blissful topic join one of my mentors, Mastin Kipp on his journey towards healing the world with his daily blogjoin us at http://thedailylove.com

Acknowledgments

I thank God for being my source of inspiration. Thanks to my mother Rebecca E. Ogwu to whom the book is dedicated. Thanks to my Special Friend Deborah L. Gonzalo for her supreme intellect, support, guidance, and daily encouragement. A special thank you to Ash, Leo , Ari and Abigeal for the smiles, love, light and Laughter on this journey. A special thank you to Rev Fr. Nkem Boniface Anusiem for his dedicated time and efforts in proof reading this book and daily prayers. Thanks to the Wandsworth house of reasoning and the entire staffs and managements where this book was originally scripted. Thank you to Clare Darwish for her dedication, passion to help, time and assistance. A special thanks to my brother from another mother Muyiwa Olumodeji at Olumz Productions, for his support, time being a good team player. A wonderful thank you to Una Less for her infinite support and kindness. Thank you to Aisha Sherman for her patience in editing the first draft of this book.

A huge thank you to my mentors, Oprah Winfrey   *Super Soul Sunday * Nobel Laureate, Professor Wole Soyinka *, Donald Trump * Think like a Billionaire * Dr Wayne Dyer   * The power of Intention*   Jim Rohn   * The art of exceptional living*, Bob Proctor   * Winners Image *, T Harv Eker   * The millionaire mind Seminar* , Napoleon Hill   *Think and grow Rich*,   Mastin Kipp   *thedailylove*   Steven K. Scott   * Lesson from the Richest man that ever lived*   Earl Nightingale   * Lead the Field *   They have empowered me with their books, Videos and Live seminars. Including personal words of advice from a few of them has laid the foundation for huge success.

A final note of gratitude to the entire production team including Sophia Blake without her persistent call, faith and support in me, this book would not have been brought to millions of readers. Thank you for a great publishing done Xlibris Publishers. All readers are Leaders !

Lightning Source UK Ltd.
Milton Keynes UK
UKOW04f2013260917
309923UK00001B/56/P